W9-CHB-315

This book belongs to

_____

_____

_____

_____

To Sasha Lois Tilden,
with bubbly chuckles – T.M.

For Natalie,
the mermaid of Cairns – G.P-R.

There are lots of clown fish hiding in this book.
How many can you spot?

First published in Great Britain in 2010 by Orchard Books

No part of this publication may be reproduced, stored in a retrieval system, or transmitted
in any form or by any means, electronic, mechanical, photocopying, recording, or otherwise,
without written permission of the publisher. For information regarding permission, write to Orchard Books,
a division of Hachette Children's Books, an Hachette UK company, 338 Euston Road, London NW1 3BH.

ISBN 978-0-545-53653-0

Text copyright © 2010 by Tony Mitton.
Illustrations copyright © 2010 by Guy Parker-Rees.
All rights reserved. Published by Scholastic Inc.,
557 Broadway, New York, NY 10012,
by arrangement with Orchard Books, a division of
Hachette Children's Books, an Hachette UK company.
SCHOLASTIC and associated logos are trademarks
and/or registered trademarks of Scholastic Inc.

12 11 10 9 8 7 6 5 4   13 14 15 16 17 18/0

Printed in the U.S.A.   40

First Scholastic printing, May 2013

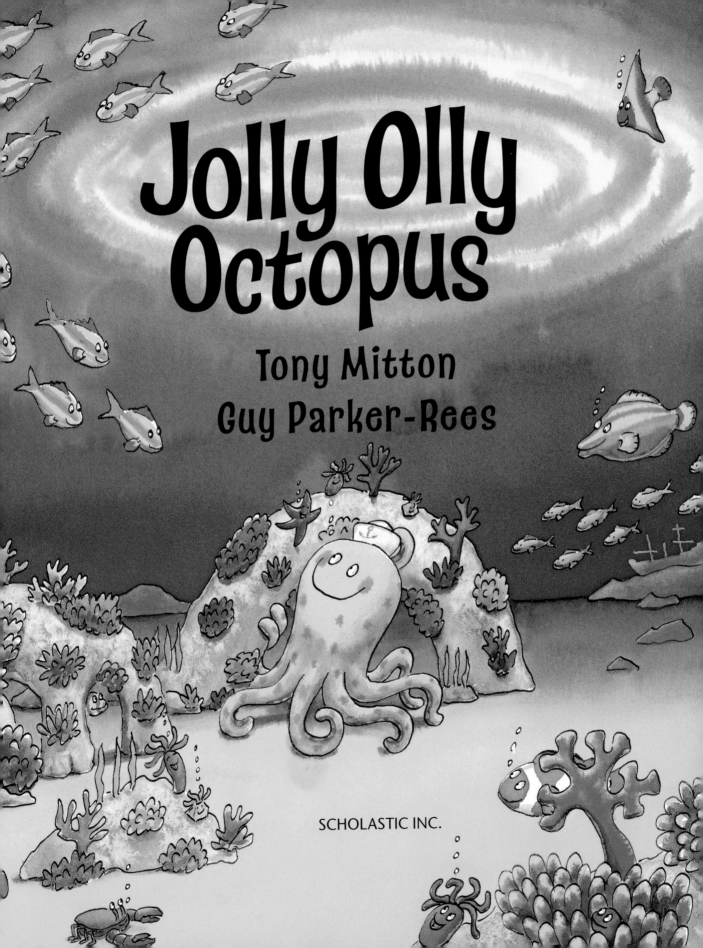

Jolly Olly Octopus

Tony Mitton
Guy Parker-Rees

SCHOLASTIC INC.

Underneath the ocean, down beneath the sea,

one wriggly octopus is giggling with glee.

Jolly Olly Octopus laughs away his troubles.

Wriggle-wriggle-giggle – what a lot of bubbles!

Two tickly turtles paddle close by.

They see Jolly Olly. They wave and say, "Hi!"

Jolly Olly Octopus
wriggle-wriggle-wriggles . . .
two tickly turtles both get the giggles!

Giggle-giggle-giggle! Tee-hee-hee!
What a lot of laughter
underneath the sea.

Three smiley sea horses idle on the tide, drifting on the current. See how they glide.

Two tickly turtles, one wriggly Olly,

three smiley sea horses — everybody's jolly!

Four loopy lobsters in a clacky band,
scuttling together across the soggy sand.

They see Jolly Olly dancing in the deep . . .
they all fall together
in a clicky-clacky heap!

Giggle-giggle-giggle! Tee-hee-hee!
What a lot of laughter underneath the sea.

Five funny flatfish start to feel flappy.
They flip about, they flop about —
everybody's happy!

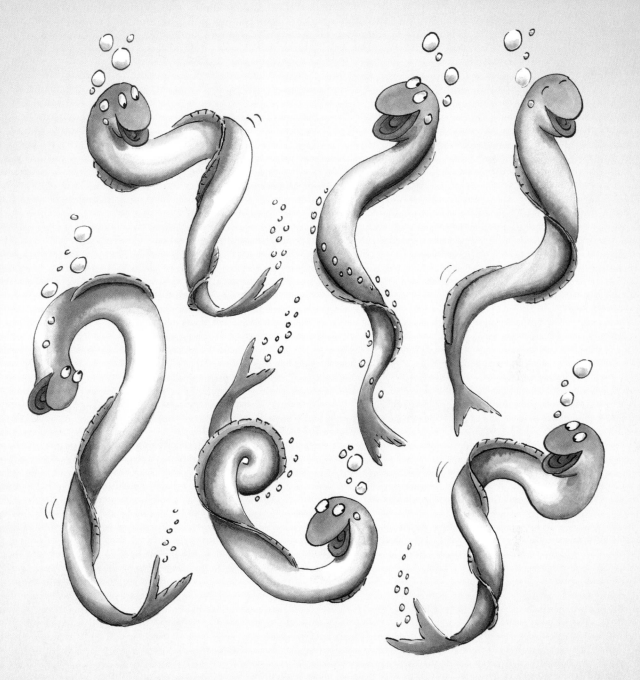

Six silly sand eels twist themselves around.
They wriggle and they jiggle
to the bubbly laughter sound.

Seven speedy sea lions come to join the fun.
They turn slippy somersaults one by one.

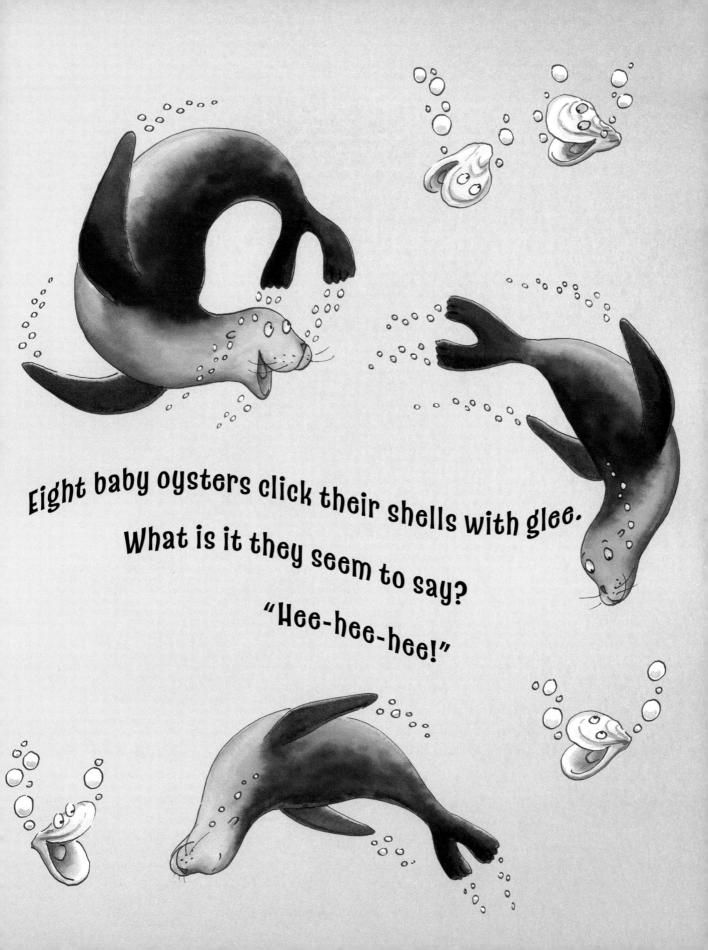

Eight baby oysters click their shells with glee.
What is it they seem to say?
"Hee-hee-hee!"

Nine nifty nautiluses start to jig and grin.

Ten dippy dolphins can't keep their giggles in.

Giggle-giggle-giggle! Tee-hee-hee!
What a lot of laughter underneath the sea.

The giggles turn to shrieks
and the laughter turns to shock . . .

Olly's in a tangle and the eels are in a tizzy.
There's flapping and there's floundering.
The water's getting **fizzy.**
They get in such a fluster as they all start to flee . . .

. . . that Shark finds them funny.

Tee-hee-hee!

The laughter swells inside him
till Shark begins to quiver . . .

so bit by bit the creatures see

they have no need to shiver.

Olly starts to caper across the ocean floor . . .

then everybody bursts out in one great . . .

FAW!

Giggle-giggle-giggle!
Tee-hee-hee!
What a lot of laughter underneath the sea.